BARNABY

WRITTEN BY
Andrea Curtis

ILLUSTRATED BY
Kass Reich

OWLKIDS BOOKS

IN A FALLING-DOWN HOUSE
on the edge of a park lived a
beautiful blue budgie named Barnaby.

His cage was gold and shaped like
a gumdrop castle. He had a swing
and a ring, a rope to chew, and bells
that jingle-jangled.

A kind lady fed him sunflower seeds
and pieces of sweet mango.

Each morning when the lady
took the quilt off his cage,
Barnaby warbled his song,
a handful of chirps like a
bubbling stream.

At night when she came
home, she let him out
so he could fly around
the room, landing here
and there, nuzzling his
feathers against her neck.

One day, the lady appeared carrying a small cage.
"I've found a friend for you." She smiled.

Barnaby turned his back.

Ack!
Ack!
Ack! he cried.

He tore at the newspapers covering the bottom of his cage. He hung upside down until he was dizzy. He squawked until the lady took the bird away.

But the next morning,
the small cage was back.

Barnaby ignored the
little yellow puff.

The lady was patient.
Each day she let
Barnaby nuzzle her
neck with his feathers.

She also talked gently to the
yellow bird, and offered him
seeds and slices of tangerine.

On the third evening, when she let him out,
Barnaby flew to her favorite pillow and began
to pull at the threads with his sharp beak.

The lady's face turned as red as her hair,
and she shut him in his cage.

The lady's voice tugged at him,
but Barnaby did not look back.

Barnaby rested on a long wooden
fence, silence heavy on his wings.

Suddenly, the flock of tiny birds filled the air
with their chirping song. They landed on the ground
nearby, flapping their wings and throwing dust into the air.

Barnaby turned his back on the dirty birds. He carefully
groomed his feathers, then pranced along the fence.

The birds ignored him, bickering
happily over seeds.

Barnaby began to whistle, amazing
even himself with the beautiful sound.

Still the flock paid him no
mind, leaving without warning
to splash in a nearby puddle.

This time when the birds moved,
Barnaby followed.

But Barnaby did not forget the kind lady.
He did not forget the little yellow bird.

Each night when darkness settled, he sang
farewell to his flock and searched for the
falling-down house.

He cruised high and low, marking his path as his friends had taught him.

And one night, there it was.

Barnaby peered through the wide-open window.
He could see the lady getting ready for bed.

He could see the yellow bird on a swing,
feathers soft as summer wind.

And there was his golden cage, the door flung
open as if he might return at any moment.

But instead of flying inside, Barnaby launched himself off again.

He flew back to the berry bush and
plucked the juiciest fruit he could find.

He carried it straight to the yellow bird's cage
and dropped the berry inside the door.

Then he nudged it in with his beak and warbled
out a warm trill to say that he was home.

For brother Ben — A.C.

*To Percival, the blue budgie I had as a kid who
was small in size and huge on personality — K.R.*

Owlkids Books acknowledges the financial support of the Canada Council for the Arts, the Ontario Arts Council, the Government of Canada through the Canada Book Fund (CBF) and the Government of Ontario through the Ontario Creates Book Initiative for our publishing activities.

Published in Canada by
Owlkids Books Inc.
1 Eglinton Avenue East
Toronto, ON M4P 3A1

Published in the United States by
Owlkids Books Inc.
1700 Fourth Street
Berkeley, CA 94710

Library and Archives Canada Cataloguing in Publication

Title: Barnaby / written by Andrea Curtis ; illustrated by Kass Reich.
Names: Curtis, Andrea, author. | Reich, Kass, illustrator.
Identifiers: Canadiana 2020028083X | ISBN 9781771473705 (hardcover)
Classification: LCC PS8605.U777 B37 2021 | DDC jC813/.6—dc23

Library of Congress Control Number: 2020941077

The artwork in this book was done using gouache paint and coloured pencil with final touches added digitally.

Edited by Karen Li and Karen Boersma
Designed by Karen Powers

Manufactured in Shenzhen, Guangdong, China, in October 2020, by WKT Co. Ltd.

Job #20CB0768

A   B   C   D   E   F

ONTARIO ARTS COUNCIL
CONSEIL DES ARTS DE L'ONTARIO
an Ontario government agency
un organisme du gouvernement de l'Ontario

Canada Council
for the Arts

Conseil des Arts
du Canada

Canadä

 Publisher of Chirp, Chickadee and OWL
www.owlkidsbooks.com | Owlkids Books is a division of bayard canada